THE ICE CREAM VANISHES

JULIA SARCONE-ROACH

Alfred A. Knopf   New York

Keep your eye on the acorn.
I'm Squirrel.
I'm a natural at making snacks disappear.
Exceptional at eating them.
Brilliant at hiding them.
And as soon as I figure out
the right magic words,
I'll be the Amazing Squirrel,
Vanisher of Snacks—
BY MAGIC!

I just need to sniff out the right snack
and the right magic words.

Abracadabra!

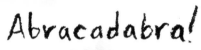

I've tried many different snacks.

I've chattered every magic
word I could think of.
And did all my fanciest
tail swishes.

But no luck.
The acorn doesn't budge.

Presto!

Acorn-o begone-o!

Scoot, scurry, scram!

By the swoosh
of my tail!

Please?!

Just then, a song jingled through the trees.
And that is when I saw it.

It is soft and cold.
Like a sweet summer snowball.
This is ice cream!
A chill zips down my tail.
Could *this* be magic?

This might be the snack I've been looking for.

I know *just* who
can help me make
it disappear.

I scamper to our spot and find the
warm lump snoring in the sunshine.
I set down the ice cream.

Waking Bear takes
all four paws.

But when we turn around, the ice cream is gone!
"I put it right here! On this hot rock
in the sun! It's vanished!"

There could be only one explanation . . .
I was a magician at last!

Could we find more ice cream to disappear?

My nose twitches. My ears prick up.

I hear the faraway call of the ice cream.

We follow the song.
It stops, but we keep going.

It leads us to a cave full of
snacks to practice magic on.
And hats. Piles of
top hats and party hats.

I'm excited to try again.
I hope I can do it.

Bear is ready
to put on a show.

STEP RIGHT UP! STEP RIGHT UP!
Birds and bugs! Rodents and reptiles!
Furry, feathery, scaly creatures of all kinds!
Direct from the branches above, it's . . .
THE AMAZING SQUIRREL,
Vanisher of Snacks, here to dazzle you
with an act so incredible,
it must be seen to be believed!

"Prepare to be astounded! Feast your eyes on this beautiful and delicious ice cream. Watch as my assistant, Bear, covers it with the mystical napkin.

Listen as I say the magic word—

abracadabra!

And then, behold . . .

The ice cream vanishes!"

Except it didn't.

Maybe the ice cream didn't hear me.
Maybe that wasn't the right magic word.
I try again.

Ice cream cone-o begone-o!
By the swoosh of my tail!

Presto!

Scoot, scurry, scram!

Please?!

Still no.

What had I said to make the
ice cream vanish before?

I took a deep breath,
remembered the sunshine
and the snoring.

I had it!

WAKE UP, BEAR!
You've got to
try this!

Don't ask me how it's done.
A good magician never reveals their secrets.
But a great magician always shares the snacks.

The show was such a hit that everyone wanted
to make things disappear.

Inside there were icy crunchers
for the raccoons.

Sweet snowballs for the bunnies.
Shivery drippers for the birds.
And so many hats.

It turns out that we were *all* good at magic.

Once every crumb, drop, and
sprinkle had disappeared,

everyone left with a
belly full of magic,
a tale of adventure,
and a party hat.

I tuck one last treat
away for later,
burrow into Bear,
and, between snores,
we mutter magic words.

And when we woke up, once again—
the ice cream had vanished!

But I wasn't surprised.
I am the Amazing Squirrel.
And together, Bear and I are very
good at making snacks disappear.

So good we could even
do it in our sleep.

THIS IS A BORZOI BOOK PUBLISHED BY ALFRED A. KNOPF
Copyright © 2023 by Julia Sarcone-Roach
All rights reserved. Published in the United States by Alfred A. Knopf, an imprint of
Random House Children's Books, a division of Penguin Random House LLC, New York.
Knopf, Borzoi Books, and the colophon are registered trademarks of Penguin Random House LLC.

Visit us on the Web! rhcbooks.com
Educators and librarians, for a variety of teaching tools, visit us at RHTeachersLibrarians.com

Library of Congress Cataloging-in-Publication Data is available upon request.
ISBN 978-0-593-30985-8 (trade) — ISBN 978-0-593-30986-5 (lib. bdg.) —
ISBN 978-0-593-30987-2 (ebook)

The illustrations in this book were created using acrylic paint, gouache, and pen and pencil.
Book design by Sarah Hokanson

MANUFACTURED IN CHINA
10 9 8 7 6 5 4 3 2 1   First Edition

For Mike, Allie, and Sydney